Green Valley Christian Preschool
376 South Green Valley Road
Watsonville, CA 95076

W9-BMP-079

To my little Nadine,
and to her dear papa.

Pili Mandelbaum

First American Edition 1990 by Kane/Miller Book Publishers
La Jolla, California

Originally produced in Belgium under the title *Noire Comme Le Café, Blanc Comme La Lune*
by Pastel, L'Ecole Des Loisirs, Paris.

Copyright © 1989 L'Ecole Des Loisirs, Paris, France
American text copyright © Kane/Miller Book Publishers

First American paperback, 1993

Library of Congress Cataloging-in-Publication Data

Mandelbaum Pili
You be me, i'll be you

Translation of: Noire comme le café, blanc comme la lune
Summary: A brown-skinned daughter and her white father experiment to see
what it would be like to have the other's skin color
[1. Fathers and daughters – Fiction. 2. Blacks – Fiction.] I. Title
PZ7.M31225Yo   1990   [E]   89-24484

ISBN 0-916291-47-2 (pbk)

Printed and bound in Singapore by Tien Wah Press Pte. Ltd.
3 4 5 6 7 8 9 10

YOU BE ME

I'LL BE YOU

Pili Mandelbaum

A CRANKY NELL BOOK

Kane/Miller
BOOK PUBLISHERS

"What's the matter, Anna?" her father asked. "Are you feeling sad?"
"No, Daddy."

"I'm not sure you're telling me everything," said her father.
"It's . . . it's just that I don't like it when people look at me," Anna finally admitted.
"But, why?" he asked.
"Because I'm not pretty."

"Not pretty? Why, you're beautiful."

"But Daddy, I don't like the color of my face, or of my hands or of my arms. I want to be like you."

"How silly," her father said. "I would do anything not to have this pale face of mine . . . pale just like the moon! Now let's see . . ."

"If we mix a bit of this color with a little of that color . . . that's it, now we have a nice brown. Wait a minute, I have an even better idea," her father announced.

"Let's make coffee-milk!" he suggested.
"Oh yes, Daddy, with lots of milk!"

"Now where are the coffee-filters?"

"Mommy is like the coffee, isn't she?" Anna said.

"And you are like the moon . . . no, like the milk!
And me? I'm like the coffee-milk!"

"Put in a little more milk, Daddy."
"No, that's enough; now it's exactly your color."

"Why aren't you drinking, Anna?
What's the matter?"

"I want to have hair like yours, Daddy."
"You must be joking," he replied.
"My hair's as straight as a board."

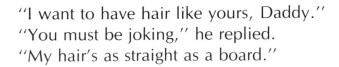

"Suppose we trade heads?" her father suggested.

"There's nothing better than coffee grounds to add some color," he said as he applied the grounds to his face.

"But how are you going to color me, Daddy?
With coffee grounds too?"
"That's going to be a surprise, Anna."

"Now help me. Spread it all over, and don't forget my neck," said her father.

"That's great. And the braids you made look terrific on me."

"Now it's your turn, Anna. I'm going to use flour to color your face.
And in a moment you'll look just like a little mime."

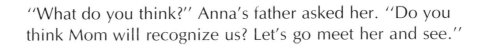

"What do you think?" Anna's father asked her. "Do you think Mom will recognize us? Let's go meet her and see."

"May I wear your hat?" Anna asked.

"Now she's really going to think I'm you," Anna said with great delight.

"Yes, you be me!" exclaimed her father.
"And I'll be you!" shouted Anna.

"Look, is there a circus or something in town?," a young girl asked her grandfather as they passed Anna and her dad on the sidewalk.

"Mom!," yelled Anna.

"What in the world are you two up to now?" Anna's mother wanted to know. "Here, just look after the shopping bags while I go to buy the bread."

"I don't think Mom likes our idea very much," said Anna to her father.
"Maybe we embarrassed her," said her father.

"Look at all those women having their hair curled . . . and those having the curls taken out," observed Anna as she pointed to women in a nearby beauty parlor. "No one seems happy with the hair they have," said her father . . .

". . . nor with the color of their skin," he added.

"And now, you two clowns, it's time you both took a shower,"
said Anna's mother when they all arrived back home.

"Tell me, Mom, do you know what you get when a piece of moon falls into a cup of coffee?" asked Anna.
"You get *pluff*," answered her mother.
"No," said Anna, "you get *me*!"

RAIN, RAIN, SMURF AWAY

by Peyo

based on the story *Le Schtroumpfeur de pluie* written by Peyo

illustrated by Peyo

Simon Spotlight

New York London Toronto Sydney New Delhi

It had rained every day for a week straight in Smurf Village. The awful weather was making everyone feel sad and gloomy.

Hmm. Everyone complains about the weather, but no one ever does anything to smurf it, thought Handy Smurf one morning. Suddenly, he had a brainstorm and hurried over to draw up his plans.

After many hours, Handy's idea began to take shape. He had created a machine that ran on floodwater.

Handy invited all the Smurfs to see his invention. They huddled together in the pouring rain.

"Now watch closely," Handy said. "I just smurf this lever, and a door will open in the roof. A wooden Smurf wearing a bathing suit will appear!"

Immediately, the clouds disappeared, and bright sunlight filled the sky. All the Smurfs jumped for joy and shouted, "Hooray!"

But when Handy pushed the lever back, a wooden Smurf carrying a mushroom umbrella appeared. Instantly the rain returned!

Handy pushed another lever that released a strong wind. "Handy, your invention is smurf-tastic," yelled Papa Smurf. "But please, smurf back the nice weather!"

To celebrate the beautiful weather, the Smurfs decided to have a big picnic.

Poet Smurf was so inspired he began writing a new poem, "An Ode to the Sun."

Everyone was having a great time and enjoying the sunshine. Everyone that is, except Farmer Smurf. He was unhappy because his vegetables were wilting!

"What my vegetables need is a nice, smurfy little shower," he said. So he set off to find Handy's weather machine.

Suddenly the beautiful weather disappeared as quickly as it had begun. Rain poured down, even harder than before.

"Oh no! I need good weather to finish my poem," Poet Smurf said.
And he set off to find Handy's weather machine too.
Poet Smurf had just brought the sunshine back
when Farmer Smurf appeared, demanding the rain.

"Rain for my lettuce!" Farmer Smurf shouted.

"Sunshine for my poem!" Poet Smurf yelled back.

The two argued while pushing and pulling on the levers of the weather machine.

BOOM! Suddenly the weather began changing from one second to the next! Rain turned into sunshine and then into a blizzard!

Hmm. Something isn't smurfing quite right with my machine, Handy thought. *I'd better go check it out.*

Meanwhile, Poet Smurf and Farmer Smurf were still fighting. But the fight ended when thick black smoke began to pour out of the weather machine.

"We're not going to be able to smurf this by ourselves," said Farmer Smurf. "We need to go find Handy Smurf!"

On their way, they met Handy, who was heading toward the weather machine. "What's going on?" he asked.

"We used your machine. I'm sorry. I think it's a little bit smurfed," Poet Smurf said sadly.

"Oh no!" Handy exclaimed. "We have to stop this before it smurfs a catastrophe! Let's go find Papa and fix the weather machine!"

Handy, Farmer Smurf, and Poet Smurf found Papa and some others and hurried back to the weather machine. But on their way, a very strong wind blew a huge tree trunk into the river. Just as they were about to cross a bridge, the tree smashed into it, and the bridge broke into pieces.

"Hurry!" yelled Papa Smurf. "We're going to have to smurf a big detour to reach the weather machine."

Just then, it got very foggy. The Smurfs couldn't see their noses in front of their faces!

The weather continued to change as the Smurfs made their way to the machine. One minute it was raining, the next it was snowing, and the next there was a thunderstorm!

When the Smurfs finally reached the weather machine, they were caught in a hurricane that swirled and blew them around like bits of straw.

Handy was able to reach the levers but he could not stop the machine. Then he smurfed an idea. He asked Brainy for his umbrella, made it into a kite, and tied the string to the weather machine.

All of a sudden, lightning hit the kite, traveled through the long string, and smashed the weather machine to pieces!

It wasn't long before the weather calmed down and everything returned to normal.

"I'm sorry about your weather machine," Papa Smurf said to Handy. "But it's just too dangerous to try and smurf rain and sunshine whenever we want it."

Handy was sad, but he knew what Papa Smurf said was true.

Poet Smurf was in the mood to write again. But now that the weather was sunny, he missed the rain.

I love the rain! I'm going to smurf a poem about the rain! he thought.

To get inspired, Poet Smurf wanted a spring shower. But he decided he **didn't** need a fancy weather **machine**—a little watering **can** worked just fine!